W9-AZD-404

Home for the Holidays

By Sonia W. Black
Illustrated by Joy Allen

Hello Reader! — Level 1

SCHOLASTIC INC.
New York Toronto London Auckland Sydney
Mexico City New Delhi Hong Kong Buenos Aires

Christmas is coming!

Christmas is coming!

We'll have fun—

at home for the holidays.

Dear Family and Friends of Young Readers,

Learning to read is one of the most important milestones your child will ever attain. Early reading is hard work, but you can make it easier with Hello Readers.

Just like learning to play a sport or an instrument, learning to read requires many opportunities to work on skills. However, you have to get in the game or experience real music to keep interested and motivated. Hello Readers are carefully structured to provide the right level of text for practice and great stories for experiencing the fun of reading.

Try these activities:

- Reading starts with the alphabet and at the earliest level, you may encourage your child to focus on the sounds of letters in words and sounding out words. With more experienced readers, focus on how words are spelled. Be word watchers!
- Go beyond the book — talk about the story, how it compares with other stories, and what your child likes about it.
- Comprehension — did your child get it? Have your child retell the story or answer questions you may ask about it.

Another thing children learn to do at this age is learn to ride a bike. You put training wheels on to help them in the beginning and guide the bike from behind. Hello Readers help you support your child and then you get to watch them take off as skilled readers.

— Francie Alexander
Chief Academic Officer,
Scholastic Education

For Vilma, with love — and thanks
— S.W.B.

To my big, crazy, loud, and wonderful family
— J.A.

No part of this publication may be reproduced in whole or in part, or stored in a retrieval system, or transmitted in any form or by any means, electronic, mechanical, photocopying, recording, or otherwise, without written permission of the publisher. For information regarding permission, write to Scholastic Inc., Attention: Permissions Department, 557 Broadway, New York, NY 10012.

ISBN 0-439-47112-5

Text copyright © 2002 by Sonia W. Black.
Illustrations copyright © 2002 by Joy Allen.
All rights reserved. Published by Scholastic Inc.
SCHOLASTIC, HELLO READER, and associated logos
are trademarks and/or registered trademarks of Scholastic Inc.

Library of Congress Cataloging-in-Publication Data available.

12 11 10 9 8 7 6 5 4 3 2 3 4 5 6 7/0

Printed in the U.S.A. • First printing, November 2002 • 24
Book design by Mark Freiman

Yippee!

We go to pick out a tree.

I think we got the best one of all!

Christmas

We hang the stockings.

Then we string lights all around.

All done!

Off we go to the mall!

We shop and shop

and shop some more.

PUPP
SALE

I take a picture with Santa.

"Cheese!" I say,

and give a big smile.

It's time to wrap the gifts

we bought!

Look at me.

I'm trying to be neat.

On Christmas Eve,
we sing carols
together.
I sing along—
I know all the songs.

Hurray! It's Christmas day!

We open our gifts.

Everyone says, "Thank you.

Thank you so much!"

In the kitchen, we are mixing,

chopping,

peeling,

baking,

cooking good things to eat.

Mmm-mmm! Yum, yum!

Now here comes

my whole family.

Lots of hugs and kisses for me!

The table is all set.

We sit.

We give thanks.

Then we eat!

After dinner, we open more gifts!

We talk.

We laugh.

We play.

And before everyone says
good-bye,
we take a picture of our
happy family.

We've had such fun—

at home for the holidays!